TICKLES TABITHA'S CANCER–TANKEROUS MOMMY
By Amelia Frahm
Illustrated by Elizabeth Schultz

Published by:
Nutcracker Publishing Company
Children's Books Adults will want to Crack Open®
P.O. Box 486, Hutchinson MN 55350
nutpubco@hutchtel.net
www.nutcrackerpublishing.com
1-888-842-8484

Special thanks to:
Professor Joann Ludeman Yost, Bethel College, St Paul, MN
Who edited this book and whose own mother died of cancer.

Writer/Author, Kay J. Johnson, Windmills and Fireflies, The Legacy of Les C. Kouba.

Hope for Today, Cancer Support Group, Maryville, TN

Hutchinson Cancer Support Group, Hutchinson, MN

Charla McMichael, R.N., B.S.N. Oncology, University of Michigan Hospital, Ann Arbor, MI

Penny Morton, R.N. B.S.N. Memorial Mission/St. Joseph's Health Care System, Ashville, NC

Laura Toperzer, age 9, Children's Book Expert

Tickles Tabitha's Cancer-tankerous Mommy/Amelia Frahm
FIRST EDITION
Library of Congress Catalog Card Number 00-108751
1. Juvenile/Fiction
2. Health/Education
3. Cancer

ISBN 0-9705752-0-3

TICKLES TABITHA'S CANCER-TANKEROUS MOMMY was written for my children, but it's dedicated to the man, who no matter how dumb my ideas or moody my behavior, puts up with me, my husband, Randy.
– Amelia

Thanks to– the people I love most in this world – my family
Mom, Dad, Paul, A.K. and Emily and to
Charlene and Penny for all the advice and critiques
also to the very special Keith Hurley.
– Elizabeth

Nutcracker Publishing Company
established in the Millennium year in honor of:

Laura Bouldin Karlman, 1961-2000. One of the people who championed this book, knowing she would never get to read it to her own children. Laura lost her battle with Acute Myelogenous Leukemia while a patient at M.D. Anderson Medical Center, Houston, Texas. Her honesty and sense of humor remain with us and are reflected in the pages of this book.

Before Mommy got sick on the inside, Mommy would tickle and Tabitha would giggle. They'd tickle and giggle until their faces turned pink and they were breathless. Tickles Tabitha was Tabitha's favorite game and Mommy always felt like playing it.

On the outside Mommy doesn't look sick. As long as she keeps a wig on her head, nobody would ever guess anything's wrong.
But Mommy's not exactly like most other women.

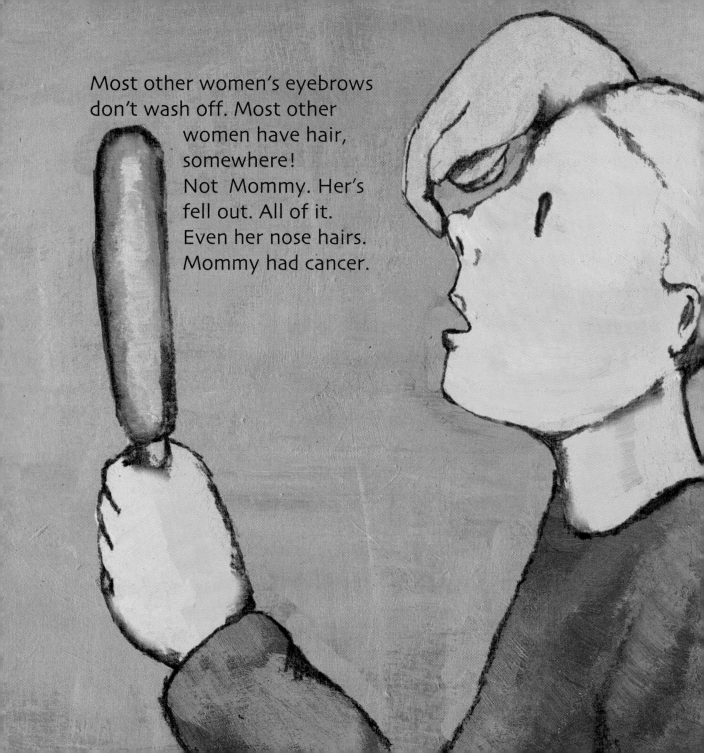

Most other women's eyebrows
don't wash off. Most other
women have hair,
somewhere!
Not Mommy. Her's
fell out. All of it.
Even her nose hairs.
Mommy had cancer.

After her operation to remove the cancer, Mommy was sad. "Does it hurt, Mommy?" Tabitha had asked.

"No I'm just scared," cried Mommy. "I want to get better, but I don't want to look like you Jeannie," she told Tabitha's baldheaded babydoll.

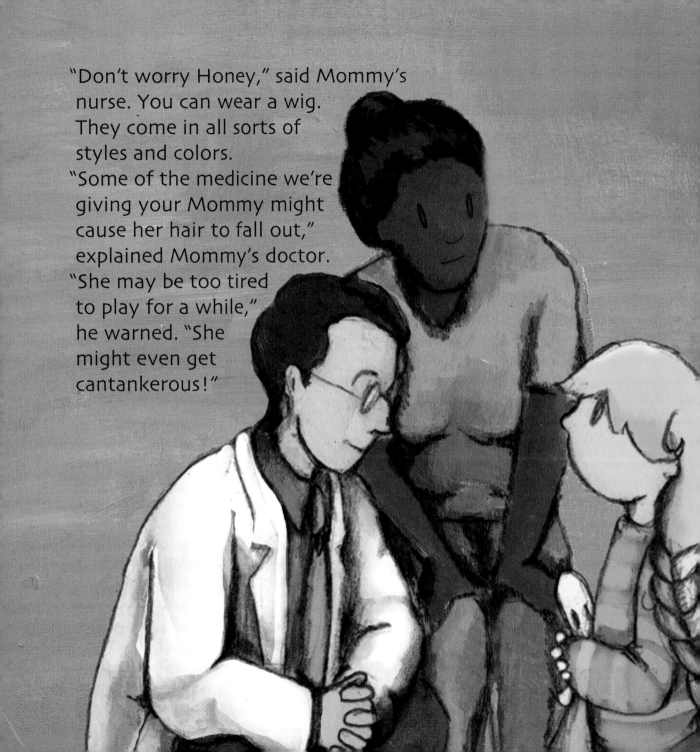

"Don't worry Honey," said Mommy's nurse. You can wear a wig. They come in all sorts of styles and colors.
"Some of the medicine we're giving your Mommy might cause her hair to fall out," explained Mommy's doctor.
"She may be too tired to play for a while," he warned. "She might even get cantankerous!"

"CANCER-TANKEROUS???"
Tabitha shrugged, all mommies with cancer probably got cancer-tankerous. She and her brother Jordan were too busy deciding what type of wig Mommy would wear to worry about that.

Mommy took her first little bitty white
medicine pill and Tabitha waited for
her to feel better.
Every morning, every night,
and once a week at the doctor's office
Mommy took her medicine.
But she didn't seem to be feeling better.

"Look at this mess," said Mommy. Tabitha
jumped up. Jordan had dumped an entire
box of cereal onto the floor and she'd
been helping him look for the prize inside.
"Go get a dustpan," Mommy told Jordan.
Mommy handed Tabitha the broom.
"Sweep up this mess," she sighed.

Mommy's wig was still on her head but she didn't look so good. The wig-hair stuck out like snarled rat-tails in all directions. There was a crooked horizontal line right where Mommy's smile should be. Worst of all, she was in no mood to play Tickles Tabitha.

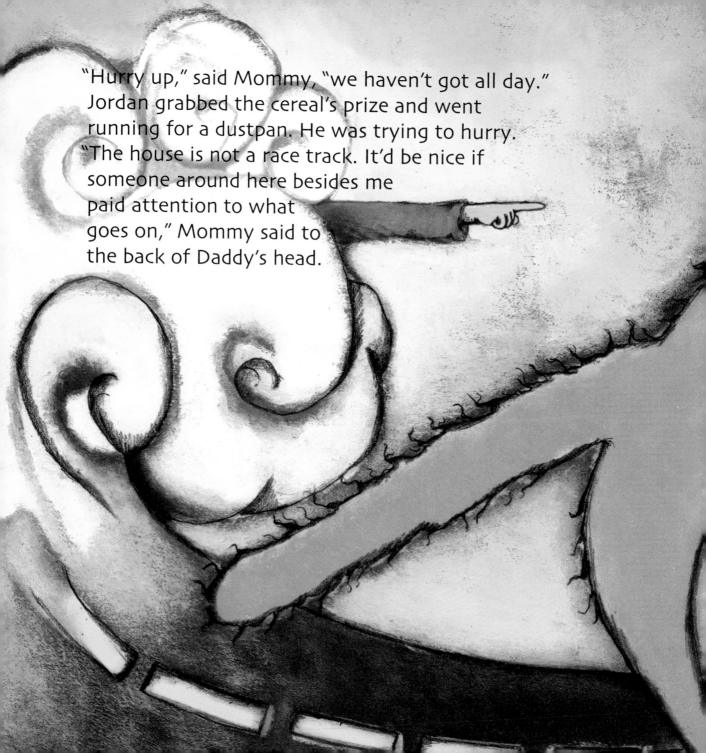

"Hurry up," said Mommy, "we haven't got all day."
Jordan grabbed the cereal's prize and went
running for a dustpan. He was trying to hurry.
"The house is not a race track. It'd be nice if
someone around here besides me
paid attention to what
goes on," Mommy said to
the back of Daddy's head.

Daddy's head nodded but only because his team made a field goal. "Doesn't Mommy's new wig look good on her?" Daddy said, without even looking. Mommy rolled her eyes. Tabitha could tell she was getting cancer-tankerous. So could Albert, their cat. He looked like a porcupine.

"Maybe Daddy needs a hearing aid and contact lenses, like Grandma Lucy," Tabitha whispered to Jordan. "Speak up, I can't hear you," Mommy complained. Tabitha knew better than to say anything, but Jordan yelled at the top of his lungs. "MAYBE YOU NEED A HEARING AID MOMMY!" Suddenly large red ears seemed to protrude from Mommy's rat-tailed wig. "Shh, you're going to burst my eardrums," Mommy whispered.

Daddy giggled, but Mommy didn't. Nothing seemed to tickle her anymore. "Don't forget to take your medicine Mommy," Daddy said.

"I wish Mommy would forget that medicine. Maybe then she'd feel like playing Tickles Tabitha," pouted Tabitha.

"Me too," agreed Jordan.

Daddy put his arms around Tabitha and Jordan. He hugged them until their heads bumped together.

"Ow," squealed Jordan.

"If you want Mommy to get better, she has to take her medicine," said Daddy. "Remember when you were sick?" he asked Jordan.

Jordan had refused to take his medicine. He said IT made him sick. So Mommy dissolved his medicine into some applesauce and fed it to him that way. Before long, Jordan was well. "Sometimes you still act sick Jordan," teased Tabitha.

"Dinner's ready," Mommy announced. Tabitha and Jordan headed straight for the kitchen, but Daddy didn't budge.
"Just a few more minutes, it's almost half-time," said Daddy.
Mommy stared at Daddy.

Tabitha eyed the timeout chair sitting in the corner. She tried to imagine what Daddy would look like when Mommy sat him there.

Mommy was hungry.
Her stomach rumbled like
a thundercloud.
The rat-tails stood
straight up and the
crooked horizontal
mouth zigzagged.
Her cheeks puffed
up like a bullfrog's.
Before Mommy could
say or yell anything,
Daddy ran into the
kitchen. He kissed
her right on her
bullfrog cheek.

"Mmmm dinner looks good Mommy," he said. Mommy didn't say one word. She just opened her zigzagged mouth so wide her face disappeared. Then she gulped down her dinner. Sometimes her medicine made her extra hungry.

Daddy reached over and tried to take a bite of Mommy's dessert. She poked him with her spoon and told him to get his own dessert. Tabitha could have sworn Mommy's nose snouted. But it was just Daddy pretending to snort like a pig. "Oink Oink."

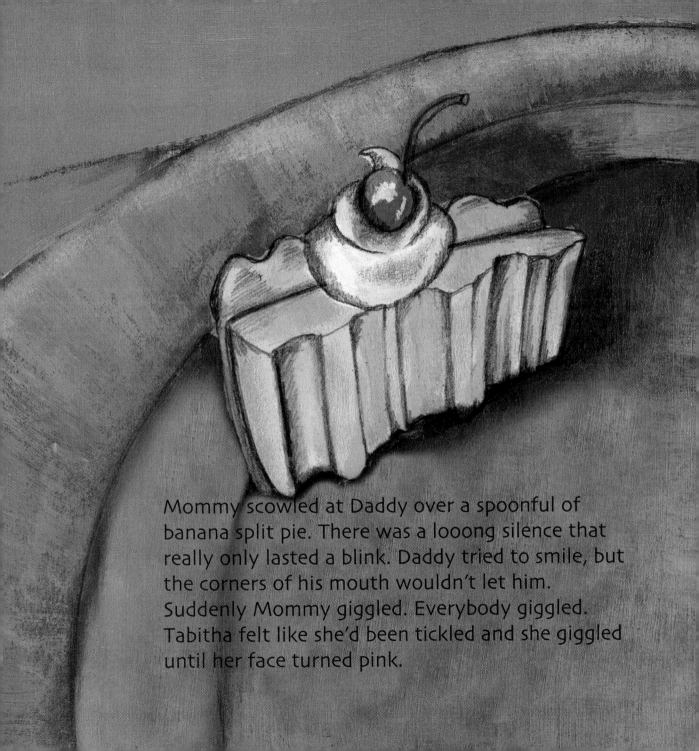

Mommy scowled at Daddy over a spoonful of banana split pie. There was a looong silence that really only lasted a blink. Daddy tried to smile, but the corners of his mouth wouldn't let him. Suddenly Mommy giggled. Everybody giggled. Tabitha felt like she'd been tickled and she giggled until her face turned pink.

That night Jordan woke up. He'd had a bad dream.
He started crying to wake Mommy. Tabitha heard him.
She got out of bed and ran to Jordan's room.
"Be quiet Jordan," she said. "Mommy's sick and tired and
you better not wake her up."
Jordan sat up in his bed, held his blankie and cried,
"Mommy, Mommy, Mommy."
Tabitha hugged her doll helplessly. "I'll get Daddy," she
said and ran to get him.

THUMP! She tripped over Albert and fell into Mommy. They both landed on the floor. Jordan quit crying and stared straight at Mommy. The tears on his chubby cheeks glistened.

"I wuv you Mommy, no matter how cancer-tankerous
you are," said Jordan.
"Me too Mommy," said Tabitha and hugged
Mommy tight. Too tight, Mommy couldn't get up.
"I love you too," Mommy gasped. "No matter
what, I'll always love you."
Then Mommy did the only thing she could
think of to get loose from Tabitha's too
tight hug. Mommy tickled her. Tabitha giggled.
She giggled until her face turned pink.
"Will you play Jickles Jordan too, Mommy?"
Jordan asked. "If you kiss me first," yawned Mommy.
Jordan lowered his head and wrinkled his nose until
his eyebrows touched. "Yuck," he said, and hid
under his blankie.

Tabitha and Mommy giggled until
their faces turned pink.